When Shere Khan, the man-eating tiger, returns to the jungle, it is no longer safe for Mowgli to live there. He sets off with Bagheera, the panther, to go in search of the man-village. But the journey is long and they have many exciting adventures as they travel through the jungle.

British Library Cataloguing in Publication Data
Disney, Walt
   Walt Disney's The jungle book.—(Ladybird
   Disney series no. 845; 3)
   I. Title   II. Kipling, Rudyard. Jungle book
   813'.54[J]   PZ7
   ISBN 0-7214-0874-5

Printed in England

WALT DISNEY'S
The Jungle Book

Ladybird Books

Deep in the jungle, Bagheera the
panther was hunting. He stopped
and pricked up his ears. There was
a strange crying sound and it
seemed to be coming from the
river.

"Why, it's a man-cub!" said
Bagheera, softly. "I can't leave
him here. He will soon need some
food. Perhaps Mother Wolf will
look after him."

Mother Wolf agreed to help. "I
will raise him with my little ones,"
she said. "We'll call him Mowgli."

So Mowgli lived with the wolf
family and grew up with his wolf-
cub brothers and sisters.

One day Bagheera came with some bad news. He told Mowgli that Shere Khan, the man-eating tiger, had come back to the jungle.

"You must leave the wolf family," he said, "and go back to the man-village where you will be safe."

So they set off for the man-village but Mowgli was very sad to leave his family. They walked through the jungle for a long time. When they were tired, Mowgli and Bagheera went to sleep on a strong branch in a tall tree.

But hiding under the leaves was
Kaa, the python snake. He slithered
along the branch to Mowgli who
woke with a jump. He had never
seen such a big snake before!

Kaa's shining yellow eyes seemed
to have a magic power and Mowgli
soon fell under their spell. Kaa
moved closer and began to slowly
wind himself round and round little
Mowgli.

Just then, Bagheera woke up and
sprang at Kaa. He gave the snake a
terrible blow with his sharp claws
and sent him slithering off into the
jungle.

Mowgli snuggled up to Bagheera
and they both went back to sleep.

At dawn a terrible roar woke
Mowgli. He looked down from the
tree and saw an old elephant
marching along with his trunk held
high in the air.

"One, two! One, two!" the old
elephant called to the other
elephants, who were trying to keep
up.

The elephants' feet made a noise
like thunder. Mowgli joined in with
the marching and was so happy
that he forgot all about Bagheera
and the man-village.

The elephants marched on and on
and soon Mowgli was lost. He
began to wish that Bagheera was
with him. And then he heard a
strange humming sound.

It was a great bear – dancing, humming and eating – all at the same time! He looked so funny that Mowgli laughed loudly.

"I'm Baloo!" said the bear. "Who are you and what are you doing all alone in the jungle?"

Mowgli told his story to Baloo. "Come on, Mowgli," said Baloo. "Follow me!"

Off they went into the jungle. Soon
they came to the river and the two
new friends waded in to keep cool.
They floated gently along until
Baloo, who had done so much
dancing, humming and eating,
soon fell fast asleep.

Mowgli and Baloo didn't know
that there were hundreds of pairs
of eyes watching from the trees.
They didn't see the monkeys
waiting to kidnap Mowgli.

As Mowgli came close, the monkeys
grabbed him. Baloo woke up but
the monkeys were too quick for him
and they made off with Mowgli.

Just then Bagheera arrived. He had been looking for Mowgli. "What happened?" he asked Baloo.

"Those monkeys have carried Mowgli off to their old ruined temple," said Baloo.

"We must make a plan to rescue him," said Bagheera.

Soon, the monkeys arrived at the temple. This was the city of Louis, King of the Apes. King Louis was sitting on his throne, waiting for Mowgli.

"So you are here at last!" he said, lifting Mowgli high in the air. "Now you can tell me the secret of fire. *All* animals are afraid of it. Only man is its master."

Mowgli was very worried. He didn't know the secret of fire.

"First, we will have a feast in your
honour!" said King Louis, and he
started the dancing.

Some of the monkeys beat out the
rhythm on the tree trunks and
Mowgli soon forgot his troubles
and joined in.

Meanwhile Baloo and Bagheera
had found King Louis' temple.
Now they were watching the
monkeys from their hiding place.

"*Now*, Baloo!" whispered
Bagheera. "You start dancing and
I'll get Mowgli!" So Baloo began
to dance with the monkeys.

He was dressed up to look like a lady ape. King Louis and the monkeys didn't know that he was really Baloo, the bear!

While the monkeys danced,
Bagheera, Mowgli and Baloo made
their escape, leaving King Louis
and the monkeys far behind.

The three friends ran deep into the
jungle and soon they rested at the
foot of a tree. Mowgli fell asleep,
while Baloo and Bagheera stayed
awake to keep watch.

Next morning Baloo and Mowgli left Bagheera and went off into the jungle. They walked for a long time.

"Where are we going?" asked Mowgli. Baloo told him that they were going to find the man-village.

"No!" said Mowgli. "I want to stay here with my friends." And he ran off, crying.

Shere Khan was on the prowl in that part of the jungle. He knew that Mowgli was close. When, at last, he saw Mowgli, Shere Khan smiled and licked his lips.

Shere Khan roared and showed his teeth. He was ready to jump…but suddenly, he couldn't move.

Baloo had caught him by the tail. Shere Khan was strong and Baloo was thrown to the ground.

Then a flash of lightning struck an
old tree and started a fire. Mowgli
rushed to pick up a flaming branch
and pointed it at Shere Khan.

The tiger's eyes were wide with
terror. "You're afraid, aren't
you?" said Mowgli.

"Let me go," said Shere Khan. "I'll be good!"

"Then go and never let me see you here again," said Mowgli, sternly.

Bagheera had been watching, and
now he ran out to hug Mowgli.
They went over to Baloo who was
lying on the ground.

"He has given his life for you,"
said Bagheera, sadly.

But then Baloo rubbed his eyes and
Mowgli started to laugh. Baloo was
alive! And happily, the three went
on their way once more.

Bagheera knew that they were close
to the village. "Mowgli will want to
know how humans live in the man-
village," he whispered to Baloo.
"Come on, let's have a look!"

They reached the village and hid in
a clump of trees. Mowgli saw a
young girl walking down to the
river. She was wearing a pink dress
and was carrying a jar on her head.

"Is that a man?" Mowgli asked his friends.

"No," said Bagheera. "That's a girl!"

"A girl?" said Mowgli. "No one said anything about girls. Isn't she pretty!"

The girl knelt down by the river to fill her jar. Mowgli wanted to have a closer look.

When he reached the river the girl smiled at him. Mowgli smiled too and blushed deep red. Then the two of them went on, into the village.

Baloo and Bagheera gave a deep
sigh. They were sad that Mowgli
was going but they knew that he
would be happy in the man-village.

"Mowgli is where he belongs,"
said Bagheera. "Come on, Baloo,
let's get back to where *we* belong,
too!" Singing and humming, the
two friends walked back into the
jungle.

*HAVE YOU READ ALL THE
WALT DISNEY CLASSICS FROM
LADYBIRD?*